P9-DVI-929

My Very First Winnie the Pooh™

Pooh, the Giving Bear

Adaptation Cassandra Case Illustrated by Josie Yee

Based on the Pooh stories by A. A. Milne
(copyright The Pooh Properties Trust).

Printed in the United States of America.

First published by Disney Press, New York, NY
This edition published by Grolier Books, ISBN: 0-7172-8903-6
Grolier Books is a division of Grolier Enterprises, Inc.

"Umph!" grunted Piglet as he dragged his wagon up to Pooh's house. The wagon was loaded with stuff. Piglet knocked on Pooh's door.

"Hello, little Piglet," said Pooh when he saw his friend. "What's all that you have there in your wagon? Is it for me?"

"Oh!" Piglet giggled. "No, it's not for you, Pooh!"

MR SANDERS
RING
ALSO

"This is stuff from my house," Piglet said. "Things out of my cupboards and shelves that I'm not using anymore. I'm going to give them to Christopher Robin."

Just then Tigger bounced up.

"Hoo, hoo, hoo! Hello!" he cried.

Tigger had a full wagon with him, too.

"Hello, Tigger," said Pooh. "Are you going to give your things to Christopher Robin, too?"

"You betcha!" answered Tigger. "I found all these things I don't play with anymore. Christopher Robin asked us to bring them to him. His school is collecting stuff to give to others who need it."

"Do you have anything you don't need anymore, Pooh?" asked Piglet. "Something that someone else could use?"

"Hmmm, let me think," said Pooh. "Think, think, think."

But he couldn't think of a thing.

Just then Christopher Robin came along. "Oh, there you are," he exclaimed. "I've been looking for all of you."

"See what we've got!" called Tigger.

"Oh, good!" said Christopher Robin. "Thank you, Tigger! That's wonderful, Piglet! What about you, Pooh? Do you have anything to add?"

"Well, um . . . ," said Pooh, "I don't know. . . .

"I don't think I have anything to give away," said Pooh sadly.

"Impossibibble!" said Tigger. "There must be something."

"Let's have a look in your cupboard," suggested Piglet. "I didn't think I had anything, either, until I looked."

Pooh was very doubtful, but he led the way inside and went to open his cupboard.

"My goodness!" exclaimed Christopher Robin.

"Oh, my!" squeaked Piglet.

"Zowie!" shouted Tigger. "You givin' a home to every lost honey pot in the whole world, buddy boy?"

"Er . . . well, you never know when I might need one," Pooh said.

"Yes, but you've got twenty pots there, silly old bear!" said Christopher Robin, smiling at Pooh fondly.

"I do?" said Pooh, feeling rather pleased with himself.

"You know," said Christopher Robin, "only ten of these honey pots have any honey in them, Pooh." He was looking through Pooh's sticky collection of pots.

"Oh," Pooh replied. "How strange! Just the other day, most of them were full." Pooh thought about this for a minute. "Well," he continued, "I *do* like to keep a large supply of *empty* honey pots as well as full ones."

"Why is that, Pooh Bear?" asked Christopher Robin.

"Just in case," replied Pooh.

"In case. . . ? In case of what?" asked Piglet anxiously. Being a very small animal, Piglet was a little afraid to hear the answer. "Do you mean, in case a hungry h-heffalump comes to visit?"

"No, little Piglet!" replied Pooh. "In case I find some especially yummy honey. Because then I would need plenty of pots to store it in."

"Oh, yes, I see what you mean." Piglet felt a lot better knowing it didn't have anything to do with heffalumps.

"Yes, but Pooh," said Christopher Robin, "if you give away your ten *empty* honey pots, you'll still have ten *full* pots of yummy honey left."

"But what if I had a party?" asked Pooh. "Everyone would want some honey, so I would need a lot."

"Silly old bear," said Christopher Robin, "if you wanted to share your honey, you wouldn't need your empty pots – only your full ones."

"Yes, that's right," said Piglet. "And if we ate up all of your honey, we'd bring you some new pots of honey to make sure you had enough."

"So you don't need to keep all these empty, old, sticky pots hangin' around," Tigger added.

"Hmmm," said Pooh. He still wasn't sure he wanted to give away his honey pots. He felt as if they were friends of his. It was hard to part with even one of them.

"Just think, Pooh," said Christopher Robin. "There are others who could enjoy having a useful pot if you would share some of your empty honey pots."

Pooh thought about this. Suddenly he remembered how happy Eeyore had been when he got a honey pot for his birthday.

"They would all be as happy as I am!" cried Pooh.

Then he decided he *would* give away some of his honey pots after all. It made him feel good inside—as good as he felt when he ate the very best honey!

"Hey, Pooh-boy, didja know there's stuff left in this one?" Tigger asked as they loaded honey pots into Pooh's wagon.

"You mean . . . honey?" asked the hopeful bear.

"Oh, yech!" said Tigger. "Tiggers don't like honey."

"Well, Poohs do!" said Pooh happily. And since it was time for a smackerel anyway, Pooh sat down right then and there, and made sure the pot would be nice and clean for its new owner.